FLY GUY'S AMAZING TRICKS

Tedd Arnold

Cartwheel Books

An Imprint of Scholastic Inc.

For Ava and Jack

Library of Congress Cataloging-in-Publication Data

Arnold, Tedd, author.
Fly Guy's amazing tricks / Tedd Arnold. —First edition.
pages cm. — (Fly Guy ; 14)
Summary: Fly Guy has learned a lot of new tricks, but when he shows off at dinner time he and Buzz get into trouble—though later they prove useful.
ISBN 978-0-545-49329-1
1. Flies—Juvenile fiction. 2. Tricks—Juvenile fiction. 3. Friendship—Juvenile fiction. [1. Flies—Fiction. 2. Tricks—Fiction. 3. Friendship—Fiction.] I. Title. II. Series: Arnold, Tedd. Fly Guy ; #14.

PZ7.A7379Fo 2014
813.54—dc23

2013051319

12 11 10 9 8 7 6 5 4 3 2 1   14 15 16 17 18

Printed in China 38
First edition, September 2014

A boy had a pet fly.
He named him Fly Guy.
And Fly Guy could
say the boy's name—

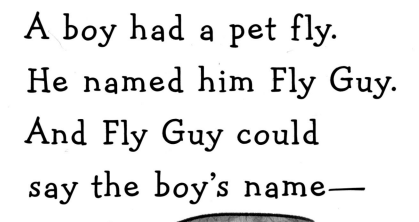

Chapter 1

Buzz's friends came to see
The Amazing Fly Guy Circus.

Buzz said, "Get ready for Fly Guy's amazing new tricks!"

"Now," said Buzz,
"The Backstroke!"

"And now," said Buzz,
"The Big Booger!"

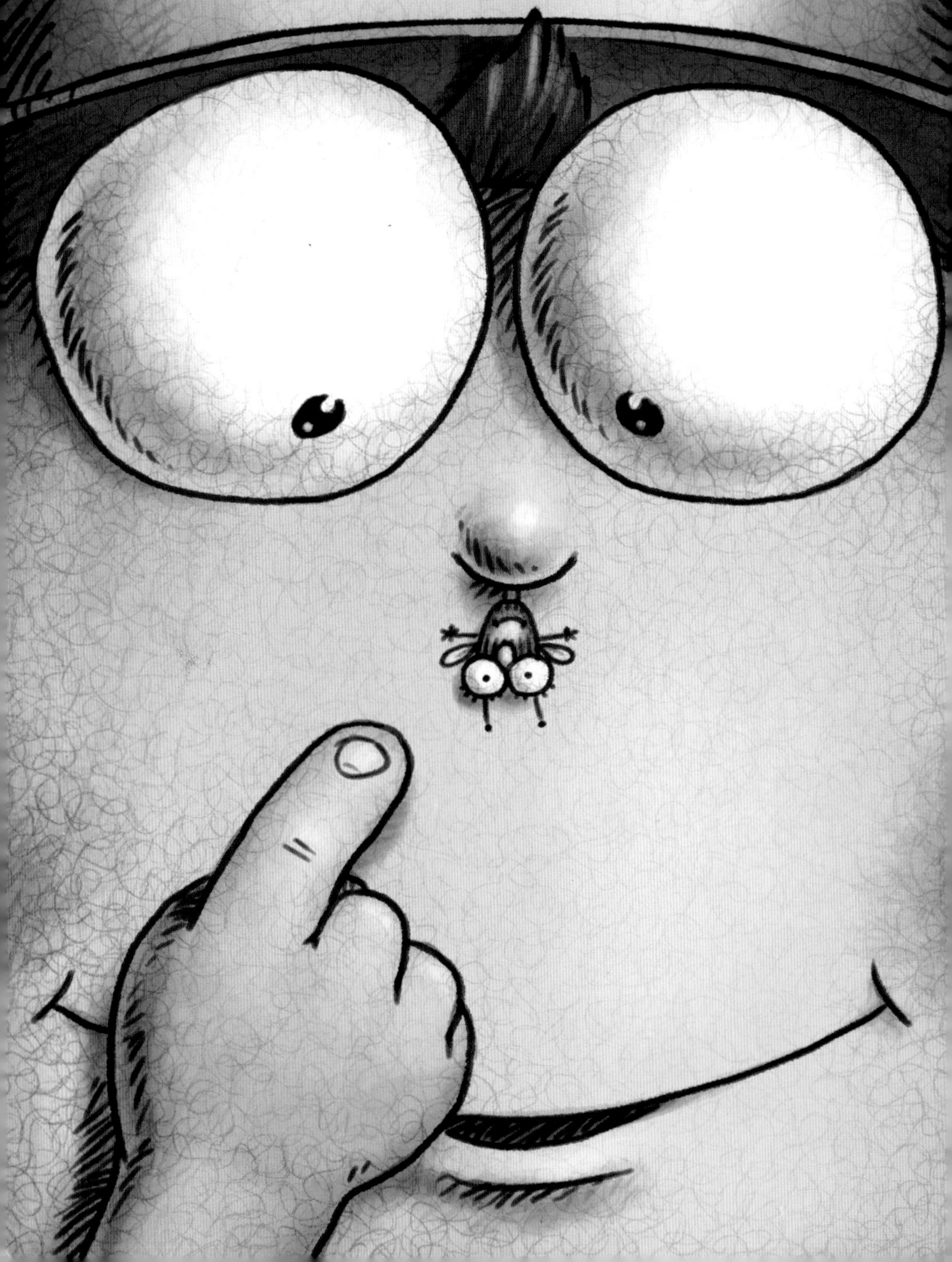

"Time for supper," said
Mom. Buzz's friends all
went home.

Chapter 2

At the dinner table, Buzz said, "Fly Guy learned new tricks."

Fly Guy did The Backstroke
in Mom's milk.

Buzz cried, "Stop, Fly Guy!"
But Fly Guy didn't hear him.

Fly Guy did The Dizzy
Doozie around Dad's head.

Buzz cried, "Stop, Fly Guy!"
But Fly Guy didn't hear him.

Fly Guy did The Big Booger.
Buzz caught him.

"Stop, Fly Guy!" he said.
"Let's clean up this mess."

Chapter 3

Outside, Buzz said to Fly Guy, "I have an idea. Do your tricks only when you hear the word NOW."

YEZZ

A big kid walked by.
He laughed. "Are you
talking to a bug?"
Buzz didn't answer.

The kid said, "Do you have bug brains?" Buzz didn't answer.

The kid said, "Bug got your tongue?" Buzz didn't answer.

Fly Guy heard the word
"NOW!"

Fly Guy did The Backstroke.

Then Fly Guy did
The Dizzy Doozie.

And then Fly Guy did
The Big Booger.

The kid yelled, "Get out of my face!"

He bumped into a garbage can.

A zillion angry flies chased
the big kid away.

Buzz said, "Fly Guy, here's a new trick for you."

"High Fivezzz!"

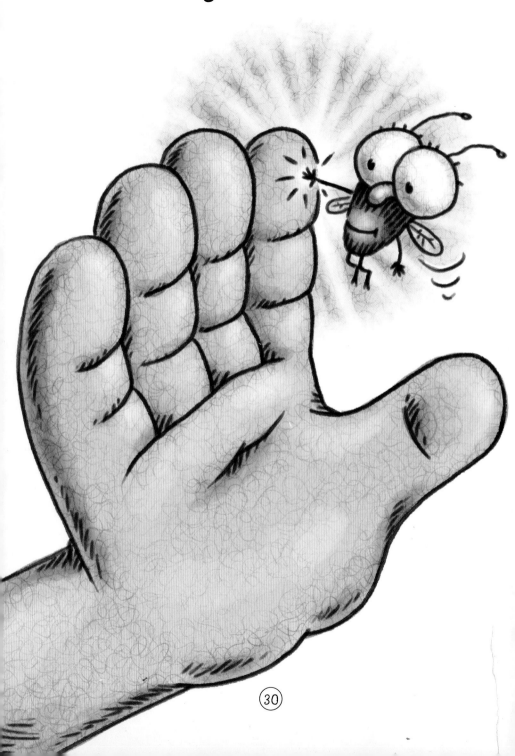